Rosie & Jii
and the Magic Sausages

Written by John Cunliffe
Illustrated by Celia Berridge

A Ragdoll Production for Central Independent Television

Hippo

Scholastic Children's Books,
Scholastic Publications Ltd,
7-9 Pratt Street, London NW1 OAE

Scholastic Inc.,
555 Broadway, New York, NY 10012-3999, USA

Scholastic Canada Ltd,
123 Newkirk Road, Richmond Hill,
Ontario, Canada L4C 3G5

Ashton Scholastic Pty Ltd,
PO Box 579, Gosford, New South Wales,
Australia

Ashton Scholastic Ltd,
Private Bag 92801, Penrose, Auckland,
New Zealand

First published by Scholastic Publications Ltd, 1994
This edition published by Scholastic Children's Books, 1995

Text copyright © 1994, by John Cunliffe
Illustrations copyright © 1994, by Celia Berridge

Design of Rosie and Jim puppets copyright © 1991 by Ragdoll Productions (UK)
Central logo copyright © 1989 Central Independent Television plc.
Based on the Central Independent Television series produced by Ragdoll Productions

ISBN: 0 590 55830 7

Typeset by Rapid Reprographics, London.
Printed by Mateu Cromo

10 9 8 7 6 5 4 3 2 1

It was a hungry day on the old *Ragdoll*. There were no eggs for John's breakfast.
He looked in the fridge. It was almost empty!
"Deary me," he said, "where does all the food go to? You'd think I had a family of hungry children on this boat, but there's only me!"

He went out on deck.
"What a lovely day!" he said. "What shall I put in my story today?
But never mind my story, I'll have to find some shops, or there'll be no
dinner tonight. I think I'd better make a list, then nothing will get
forgotten. Let's see, now..."
John found a piece of paper, and began making his shopping-list.
This is what he wrote:

1 loaf
2 bottles of milk
3 oranges
4 apples
5 carrots
6 eggs
7 tins of soup
8 packets of biscuits
9 tomatoes
10 fish fingers

He popped the list under his waterways book so that it would not
blow away. Then he started the engine and cast off.

Duck quacked.
In the cabin, Rosie and Jim were listening.
"We're moving!" said Rosie.
"Where are we going?" said Jim.
"Shopping," said Rosie.
"What for?" said Jim.
"Lots of lovely food," said Rosie.
"Goody," said Jim, "I'm *so* hungry."
"Oooh, greedy noggin," said Rosie, "you had the last egg for your
breakfast, and there were none left for poor old fizzgog."
"I'm still hungry," said Jim.
"He's made a list," said Rosie.
"Let's have a look," said Jim.

He borrowed John's list, when he wasn't looking.

"Oooh, fizzy old noggin, look at this," said Jim. "No sausages, *again*!"

"And," said Rosie, "no toffee yoghurt."

"I do like sausages," said Jim.

"I do like toffee yoghurt," said Rosie.

"Let's..."

"Put them..." said Jim.

"On John's list!" said Rosie.

"How do you spell toffee yoghurt?" said Jim.
"Oh, hum, well...fizzpot, you just...er...hmmm, diddle,
pop...ermmmmmm..."
"Rosie?" said Jim. "Do you *know* how to spell it?"
"No, Jim. And I don't know how to spell *sausages* either," said Rosie
sadly.

"So we can't..." said Jim.

"Yes, we can," said Rosie. "We can cut pictures out of a magazine, and stick them on John's list. Look, I'll show you."

Rosie and Jim looked through John's old magazines, until they found pictures of toffee yoghurt and of a packet of sausages. They cut them out and stuck them to the end of John's list.

"That's it," said Rosie. "Now pop it back under his book, and he'll never notice."

John soon found a good place to moor the boat. He got out his shopping-bag, and away he went. Duck quacked.

"Duck's quacking," said Rosie. "Hurry up, Jim, off we go!"
"Coming, Rosie!" said Jim.
They followed John into the town. There was a busy street full of shops.

There were shops of all kinds. There were sweet shops, television shops, book shops, newspaper shops, and shops that sold a bit of everything. John went into a small shop on the corner. Rosie and Jim peeped through the window to see what John was doing.
"Look, Rosie," said Jim, "he's giving the lady his shopping-list."

John hurried away without his shopping.
"Where is he off to?" said Rosie.
"I know," said Jim, "he's forgotten something. She's putting all his shopping in his bag, and he's going to come back for it."
"Let's stay and watch," said Rosie, "to make sure nothing gets missed."
"Specially..."
"The fizzy old toffee yoghurt," said Rosie.
"And the super sausages."
"But, Jim," said Rosie, "John doesn't like sausages."
"And he doesn't like toffee yoghurt," said Jim.
"He's going to be very very cross, when he finds them in his shopping," said Rosie.
"*Very* cross," said Jim.

"I know what we can do," said Rosie. "We can buy him a nice present to cheer him up."

"More sausages?" said Jim.

"*No, prattle-box,*" said Rosie, "that would make him more cross than ever. We'll buy him something he likes. I have a fat 50p in my bag. We can buy it with that. Let's see, what would fizzygog like?"

"Flowers," said Jim.

"Flowers? Yes. Mmmmmm. I think he would like flowers. Some nice flowers to put in the *Ragdoll*. That's a good idea, Jim, and there's a flower shop next door."

Rosie and Jim went next door to get some flowers for John. By the time they returned, he had come back for his box of shopping and they had to run to keep up with him. What a hurry he was in!

When John got back to the boat, he saw a family having a picnic by the river bank.

"That's a good idea," he said. "I think I'll have a picnic with my shopping."

So he unpacked all his shopping on a picnic table by the river. Oh, you should have seen his face when he found the toffee yoghurt and the sausages! He was just as cross as Rosie and Jim thought he would be. He was so cross that he almost threw the sausages into the river.

"Ooooh, what a silly noggin-face!" said Rosie, hiding behind a tree.
"Don't throw Jim's sausages into the river!"
You might have thought that John heard what Rosie said.
"I wonder if those people would like some sausages and toffee
yoghurt for their picnic?" said John. And he walked across the grass
to ask them.

"My sausages!" said Jim.
"My toffee yoghurt!" said Rosie.
"Now," said Rosie. "Let's pop the flowers on his table."
The people liked sausages and toffee yoghurt.
"Thank you very much," they said. "Lovely. Just the thing for the children."

"Quick," said Rosie.

Rosie and Jim ran across the grass and hid under the picnic table. They soon made friends with the children, and none of the grown-ups seemed to notice at all. When the grown-ups had cooked the sausages, the children passed them and the yoghurt under the table to Rosie and Jim, and they had a lovely picnic all of their own. When John found the flowers on his picnic table, he began to smile again. He ate a cheese sandwich, and looked much happier.

"They worked," said Rosie.

"I'm too full to talk," said Jim.

And when they all went back to the *Ragdoll*, John smiled again, because the sausages had given him an idea for his story. This is the story he wrote:

One windy day, Rosie and Jim were travelling along on the good boat *Ragdoll*.
"I'm hungry," said Jim.

"Look in the fridge," said Rosie, "and see what you can find for supper."
Jim looked in the fridge, but it was empty except for a piece of cheese that had grown old and green and furry.

"You'll have to catch a fish for your supper," said Rosie.
So Jim made a fishing line with a boat hook, a piece of string and a pin. He put the piece of mouldy cheese on the pin.
Jim plopped his line into the water. He soon shouted, "Got one!"

Jim had caught a big pink fish.
"Hello," said the fish, "I'm a magic fish. Would you like a wish?"
"A packet of sausages, please," said Jim.

"Let me go, and you can have a packet of the best sausages," said the fish.
Jim let the fish go. It swam quickly away.
"You noggin," said Rosie. "It will never come back, and we'll get no supper."

But, there on the table was a packet of sausages. Jim opened the sausages. They gave a wriggle and grew little legs. They jumped off the table. They ran away at top speed. They ran for their lives, off and away along the towpath.

"Quick," shouted Rosie, "after them!"
Rosie and Jim chased the sausages over a hill, round a corner, down
some steps, through a garden, up a passage, under a bridge, and
along a street full of shops, but they could not catch them.

"Stop," said Rosie. "They're too fast for us."

"Look," said Jim.

They were outside a little corner shop.

"We'll just have to get something for our dinner in there."

They went into the shop, and bought sausages, yoghurts, crisps, jam doughnuts, and bacon. Then they went home and had such a feast. They never saw the magic fish again, or the sausages with legs. I don't know *where* they ran to.